Beginnings

Jan McDonald

Raven Crest Books

Copyright © 2014 Jan McDonald

ISBN-13: 978-0-9933747-9-1
ISBN-10: 0-99-337479-4

THE BEGINNING

Mike Travis walked towards his waiting Wessex helicopter; towards another mission in war-torn Afghanistan.

His outward appearance was casual but inside he was anything but. Only a fool would relax at the beginning of any mission in that place.

It was early 2006 and Camp Bastion was just taking hold in the remote desert to the south of Lashkar Gah, the capital of Helmand Province. Facilities were minimal and personnel present were only too aware that they were in the heart of the theatre of war. Basic hygiene, catering and medical facilities and other essential services to support the squadron of helicopters and the engineers that were creating the base from the desert were well established, but anything more than that was a flight away.

Another airman was coming towards him dressed in a flying suit carrying his helmet under his arm. He was handsome in the classical way; tall and slim with finely carved features in olive skin. He raised his hand in greeting and grinned at Mike. His mission was over as Mike's was about to begin. Jack Carter had been a close friend of Mike's since they had undergone their pilot training together back home a few years earlier, and they had found themselves posted into the same squadron after that training. Jack's easy manner and sense of humour had quickly sealed their friendship back then, and now in the intensity of their situation the bond had strengthened.

"Hi Mike. Just off?"

Mike nodded. "Yep. Basic recon. There's been a signal giving intel that insurgents have been sighted about five miles away. Going to check it out." His tone was light but underneath was the knowledge that any mission could end

1

in his not returning. With only two days to go until the end of his tour of duty, Mike was far from complacent.

Jack nodded. "Safe trip. See you later." He put his hand out and Mike gripped it briefly and walked on.

Pre-flight checks complete and take-off cleared; Mike lifted the Westland Apache into a hover and began to taxi slowly forwards into lift. At around fifty feet up he heard the shot.

They say you never hear the shot that kills you, but if that shot hits the tail rotor of the chopper you're flying that could prove not to be the case. The first shot from the sniper hit the fuselage somewhere mid-engine, the second took out the tail rotor and the uncontrolled spin was instant. And the crash, vertical. And fast.

Mike's training had kicked in and had been instinctive and instantaneous. In a heartbeat he hit the release on his harness and leaned towards the open door. At twenty five feet he threw himself clear as his mission ended before it had begun; in the din of breaking engine and the screech of twisting metal.

It was dark and he was cold. And confused. People were yelling and then everything faded to nothing as his heart ceased its regular beat and became an almost imperceptible flutter before it stopped, and his lungs no longer sought air.

The emergency response was immediate with everyone running towards the wreckage of both the helicopter and Mike. Fire crews were straight on the scene along with the base medics and off duty personnel who stood ready to assist but were held back in case of explosion.

Mike stood on the edge of the group of people bent over something on the ground that from where he stood looked like a bloodied flying suit, and as he looked to his left he saw the wreckage of the helicopter. Some poor bastard had run out of luck. He mentally thanked God that it couldn't be Jack; a sentiment that many had experienced tinged with guilt that in being grateful for the life of one meant accepting the loss of another.

An airman clad in his flying suit stood at the periphery of the frantically working people, he was vaguely familiar and it annoyed Mike that he couldn't remember his name. Aware of the fact that he could do nothing to help whoever it was on the ground he nodded acknowledgement to the other airman and turned back towards the crew room. Jack would still be there ready for debriefing; they could maybe catch a coffee together before he got the all clear for his own mission.

Before he could move away from the scene, the familiar airman approached him. He looked serious and there was something about his pale complexion and the strange mark in the centre of his forehead that worried Mike. The guy must have been out there too long; it got to everyone in the end. Mike scanned the flying suit for the name badge. It said Wallis and his shoulder tapes told him that it was Flight Lieutenant Wallis. He still felt that the name should mean something and it made him feel uncomfortable.

He smiled at the guy, "There's nothing we can do, so best we leave it to the experts. We're just in the way here. I'm sorry, I feel like I should know you? Are you just passing through? I'm Mike Travis by the way. I'm going back to the crew room; I guess my sortie is on hold, we can wait for news back there."

The airman's solemn expression remained unchanged. "Yeah, I guess you could say I'm just passing through. My tour started eight months ago, though I'm afraid it didn't last too long. I took a direct hit the second week I was out here."

Mike looked puzzled, so the airman pointed to the mark on his forehead. "It was messier than it looks. Goddamn near took my head off, but that's not what you'd want to see, not in your state. Not yet."

The proverbial penny plummeted. Wallis. Flight Lieutenant Brian Wallis. Killed by sniper fire two weeks

3

into his tour of duty, and he'd looked familiar because Mike had seen the obituary in Squadron Standing Orders.

He suddenly felt disorientated and the extreme cold that was taking hold of him dropped another degree.

He couldn't remember returning to the crash scene but he found himself looking over the shoulder of one of the medics.

The body on the ground was covered in blood and lumps of wreckage. The left leg looked like something from a butcher's shop and was at alarming angles from the body, and a large red stain had spread across the chest where jagged bone from broken ribs protruded through the flying suit.

Mike forced himself to move his gaze up towards the head. The left cheek was covered in blood from a long, deep gash that ran the length of the cheekbone. But even through the gore he recognised his own face.

There was a sudden and massive pain in his chest and then there was only oblivion.

Jack, having been in the crew room when it happened, was one of the first non-emergency personnel at the wreck. The senior fire officer yelled at him to get back but he ignored him and ran to Mike. Again medics held him back, barking orders at him to stand clear. It only took a fragment of a second to realise why.

"Clear!" came the order, followed immediately by the jolt of electricity, that combined with the drugs that they'd shot directly into his main artery, was hoped would restart Mike's heart.

Jack felt as if his own had stopped.

"Clear!" There was a pause and then, "Again!" Another pause, and then "Again!"

Jack heard someone say "Call it," and then another voice countermanding that with, "Once more!" It seemed as though time was standing to attention in a surreal moment of tragedy, and then a voice yelled, "Got him!"

Other voices floated towards Jack but he had heard the

one phrase that mattered. He stood back as medics lifted his friend onto a stretcher and shoved it into the back of a Land Rover which left the scene in a cloud of desert dust.

As an accompanying Land Rover started up to follow, Jack jumped into the back of it. No-one protested.

Everyone in the emergency room had swung into action, calm and disciplined, implementing procedures that they had trained long and hard in, procedures that they had hoped never to carry out.

Mike opened his eyes. Masked faces haloed in bright light bent over him, and he was aware of the young nurse in dark blue scrubs who stood at his head, before the exquisite agony that filled his entire body blotted everything else from his consciousness. He tried to speak to her but couldn't frame the words let alone find his voice. He swallowed hard and locked his eyes into hers seeking any kind of comfort. The senior masked face barked an order and someone moved in close to him and emptied a syringe into a cannula in the back of his hand. The young nurse put a cool hand on his forehead and gently brushed back his hair. She smiled at him, "You're okay," she said. "You're safe now. They're evacuating you out of here. You're going home, Sir."

Blessed waves of warmth and detachment rippled through him as the sedation took effect. The young nurse turned to Flight Lieutenant Brian Wallis who had silently joined her, she smiled at him before unseen and soundless they left together.

Mike's left leg was mangled and he'd completely smashed two ribs. The doctors in the field hospital could only patch him up and keep him alive. Amputation was discussed, but the decision had been taken to risk flying him out of there, eventually to the UK military hospital unit where there were state of the art facilities and access to the best surgeons and the ground breaking skills and equipment that would be his only hope of saving his leg.

The Queen Elizabeth Hospital is just such a unit on the

outskirts of Birmingham with the largest organ transplant unit in Europe and massive single-floor critical care unit. It also housed the Royal Centre for Defence Medicine for military personnel injured in conflict zones.

Mike had been taken there sedated, a condition which was maintained in the form of an induced coma as his body fought back after the many hours of extreme surgery. The shattered bones in his leg, along with the knee joint, had been replaced with a titanium joint and 'bones', and plates and rods that allowed Mike to keep his leg. There would always be pain and there would always be a pronounced limp but he would have a functional leg. Experimental titanium ribs were pinned in place of the jagged bones and from there on in it was all about recovery and rehabilitation. All of which he was unaware of as he slept.

He was also unaware of his daily visitor who sat beside his bed for hours at a time. His squadron was home and Jack was on leave. He talked to Mike about their training days, their off duty activities, women they had dated, anything he could think of to fill the one sided conversation.

On day four they decided to lighten the sedation. It was time to start bringing Mike slowly out of the coma.

On day five Mike was breathing without the aid of the ventilator and they removed the tube from his throat. The critical care registrar installed a syringe into the huge unit at the side of the bed that steadily administered a drug into Mike's vein. He stirred. And coughed. And opened his eyes.

His recovery was swift, aided by heavy doses of opiates and regular visits from Jack and two days after he woke he was deemed ready to be moved to the main unit.

He was put into a four bedded room, two of which were empty; his companion was a bomb disposal sergeant who had lost an arm whilst defusing an IED at the roadside south of Kandahar. There had been no reconstructive surgery for him. The blast had taken his arm off and burned the side of his face and he'd undergone two operations and skin grafts with more scheduled. He didn't talk much, steeped in depression that was made suddenly worse by his fiancée ditching him. His pain and bitterness festered and he refused counselling.

It was on the third morning after moving from critical care that Mike noted a change in him. He seemed calmer, more centred and surprisingly ready to talk. Mike was only too glad to oblige and they sat talking together for over an hour about nothing that really mattered.

Their idle chat was interrupted by a nurse bringing Mike more medication. She seemed surprised to find Mike alone. "Morning, Sir. It's a lovely day, who were you talking to?"

Mike looked over at the empty bed next to him. He frowned and ignored her question. "Where's Sergeant Holmes?" he asked quietly.

Her face clouded over and she put the tray of medicines down on his locker, bending to straighten his bed and pillows before she said quietly, "I'm sorry, he died in the night."

The shock hit Mike twofold. Number one, he had just been talking to him and number two, Frank Holmes had been on the mend. He chose to ignore number one; the implications were too daunting to contemplate. He addressed number two.

"But he was getting better?"

The nurse nodded, "He was. But I'm afraid he took his own life. He was found in the bathroom by the night staff. Look, I'm afraid I can't discuss this with you, Sir. But I can get you moved to another room if you'd prefer it."

Mike shook his head too vigorously. Images of an airman with a hole in his forehead and a nurse in blue scrubs sprang into his head. He wasn't about to say anything that would put him on the psych ward. He was screwed.

UNDER THE OAK TREE

Three weeks of intensive physiotherapy and rehabilitation in the beautiful setting of Headley Court in Surrey, the Defence Medical Rehabilitation Unit, had left Mike Travis exhausted and on edge.

His anxiety had nothing to do with the titanium knee joint and plates and rods that had saved his mangled leg, after his Apache helicopter had been shot down just two days before the end of his tour of duty in Afghanistan. Nor was it to do with the constant pain that he was told would always be with him. It was more to do with something else he'd brought home with him. Something he couldn't talk about.

In the immediate aftermath of the crash, Mike had died. At least, he'd been clinically dead. The immediate response of the base medics, and their determination that they weren't going to lose another colleague to the insurgents, won the battle to save him. Brave decisions from the medical officers to airlift him home to attempt to save his leg had also proved successful.

The thing was, since Mike had woken from the induced coma that had kept him stable during the immediate recovery period, he'd discovered his 'souvenir' of the event.

He could observe and interact with inhabitants of the spirit world. In common parlance, he could see ghosts.

It had been obvious early on that he was interacting with beings that no-one else could see or hear. And that was the kicker. If no-one else could see them, and Mike disclosed his experiences, he had a pretty good idea which ward would be his next port of call. For a very long time.

So he said nothing.

In the dark silence of the middle of the night he lay in his hospital bed questioning his sanity. Had they been real? Had he really had conversations with dead people? Perhaps he really did need a bed on the psych ward.

The door to his room opened for the nurse on night duty to check in on him. He closed his eyes and feigned sleep, not wanting to talk to anyone whilst his mind was in freefall.

The light from the corridor illuminated the foot of his bed where he sensed the nurse's presence. Normally she would enter the room, check his pain level if he was awake, and bring him the necessary painkillers if it was too much for him. He tried to balance the desire for solitude with his need to quell the agony in his leg. That night he decided to allow her to leave the room as quietly as she had entered it.

Except she didn't leave.

He could sense her still at the foot of his bed, although she hadn't spoken. He kept his eyes shut.

He felt the change in the atmosphere, the sudden chill that seemed to envelop the bed, the subtle movement from the foot of the bed to beside him. And he knew before he opened his eyes that it wouldn't be the night-nurse standing there.

He prepared to reach for the call button that would bring him help, and more importantly, a sedative. His heart was racing and he was sweating. He didn't want to see what or who was standing there. Because then he would have to deal with it. He was losing his mind.

He opened his eyes.

The nurse that stood at the side of his bed was dishevelled and obviously distressed. But that wasn't the only thing that was strange. Her uniform was different to the one he had become used to seeing. Even in the half light of the room he could make out the blue-grey of the dress and the cap which was of the white, starched triangular variety, the white, starched apron and cuffs completed the picture of a post-war nurse. Her dress and apron had been torn and there were bruises on her face. As she moved her head, Mike could see the livid red mark on her throat.

He had a choice. Lose it and press the call button, which would more or less ensure his transfer to the psych ward, or go with it. He decided to go with it; images of becoming a zombie on the meds they would surely make him swallow would seal his fate.

"Who did this to you?" he asked gently.

"The young officer wounded in Aden. He was angry when I wouldn't ..." She lowered her eyes, unable to finish the sentence.

"He raped you?"

She nodded miserably and touched the livid mark at her throat. "And then he strangled me. My name is Annie Stephens. Please tell them I didn't just run away. I'm buried out there under the oak tree. His friends did that. "

He tried to take her hand in his but it simply passed through hers and settled on the crisp white sheet.

"Oh God," he whispered.

Sleep wasn't an option as she faded into the semi darkness and by the morning he had made his decision. He was going to tell the doctor what was happening to him and take the consequences.

His nurse on the day shift was a plump and cheerful girl called Sarah who breezed into his room with his morning medication.

"Good morning Squadron Leader," she said brightly. "How was your night? You can try a short walk outside in the garden later, the physio is really pleased with your progress and you'll be discharged soon." She paused as she saw the dark shadows around his eyes that were full of pain. "Here, let me help you with your meds." Her concern was obvious.

He swallowed the heavy duty pain killers and took a deep breath. "Can I see the doc when he does his rounds?

There's something I need to talk to him about."

Her demeanour became instantly professional. "Of course. Is there anything I can help you with?"

He shook his head, "No. I don't think so, thanks."

The morning dragged and around eleven he had a visit from the welfare officer who told him gravely what he already knew deep down. He was to be medically discharged from the service. He discussed Mike's pension and the support that he'd receive in a very clinical manner and left him in an even worse mood.

Mike's lunch stayed on the tray untouched and Sarah's concern deepened. At two-thirty she returned with a bright smile.

"You have a visitor," she said. "Maybe he can cheer you up."

Jack Carter appeared in the doorway behind her, his broad grin serving to emphasise the roguish twinkle in his eyes. They'd been friends since pilot training and had remained so ever since, posted to the same squadron and serving together in Afghanistan.

"Hi, Mike."

Mike couldn't help but smile at his friend despite his black mood. Jack had that effect on everyone. "Hi, yourself," he said.

"So, what's happening? They said I could take you into the grounds for a dose of sun. What do you think?" He picked up the crutches that were resting against the wall beside the bed.

Mike shook his head. He was in no mood for a dose of sun. "I'll pass if you don't mind. It's good to see you."

"I should bloody well think so. I've got a forty-eight hour pass and can think of better things to do with it than look at your sour face. You're going out into the sun with me whether you like it or not, you ungrateful bastard."

Mike laughed despite himself.

"That's more like it. Time you were out of this place, but you've got to co-operate. What will it take? A course of enemas?"

Mike laughed again. Seeing Jack was as effective as any antidepressant. He became serious all of a sudden. "They told me this morning that I'm out. Finished. Pensioned off."

"Yeah, well getting shot down, dying, and turning your leg into something that looked like chopped liver would do that." He became serious then. "Will you be all right? Financially, I mean."

Mike nodded. "I've got some savings and the pension is more than generous. That's not the issue. What the hell am I going to do with my time, Jack? I'm not cut out for being a goddamn cripple!" The bitterness in his voice lingered in the air between them.

Jack frowned. "Then fucking well get your sorry arse out of that bed and come outside with me. Come on. Move it."

Mike swung his legs painfully to the side of the bed, grinding his teeth at the crescendo of agony that shot up into his core as Jack held out the crutches for him.

Jack grinned. "Want a wheelchair?"

"Sod off."

"Charming. What would your nice nurse say?"

Jack held out his arm to support Mike as he slowly stood upright. Mike refused it.

Sarah smiled at them as they moved slowly towards the ward door. She grinned at Jack, her face coming alive. Jack had always had that effect on the female of the species, which was ironic given his natural preferences. "Not too far," she said. "He's feeling a little delicate today."

"I'll look after him, honest."

Outside, Mike straightened up and looked around at the grounds of the Cromwellian manor house. "Let's go over there," he said, nodding towards the huge old oak tree in the middle of a small grassed area.

"Na. I've got a better idea. We're going to the pub."

Mike laughed aloud then. What the hell. If he was soon

to be certified insane, he may as well have a drink first. He wondered about the effect of alcohol with his pain meds and dismissed the thought as soon as it surfaced. "You're on," he said.

"My car's over there. Can you walk that far?" Jack showed his genuine concern.

"Watch me."

"You'd better put this on; pyjamas aren't the best mode of dress for a country pub." He tossed his coat to Mike.

Getting into Jack's car proved awkward and excruciatingly painful resulting in beads of perspiration on his brow but Jack knew better than to try and help him.

The Plough was tucked away down a quiet country lane in the village of Effingham, something Mike could see the funny side of. Jack was a tonic and he began to feel more positive. So positive, that he reversed his decision to talk to the doctor about his experiences. He told Jack instead.

When he'd finished, Mike said, "What do you think? I'm crazy, right?"

"I think we need another drink. That's what I think. If you want to know if you've lost your marbles, then I don't think so. You were dead, Mike. Not many come back from that. I'm not religious or anything like that, but if you're asking me if I believe in some form of afterlife, then yeah, I do. And if you can see ghosts now, then I don't believe that anyone has the right to argue with you. There's a way to prove it anyway. Think about it while I get the drinks in - you'll be too slow!" he laughed.

Jack was wrong about one thing; there was no way to prove it. Not in any scientific way that would be beyond doubt that was. But he could prove it to himself. Maybe.

Jack put the pint in front of him. "Well, are you going to do anything about it?"

Mike took a gulp of foaming beer, "Hell, yes. A girl was raped and murdered and buried back there. She deserves some recognition of the fact. There must be some record of her. She was one of us, Mike."

Jack nodded enthusiastically, "Exactly. So, if you've stopped feeling sorry for yourself, what's your plan?"

"She just wanted the authorities to know where she was, and to be buried properly. I think an anonymous phone call to the police telling them that a body is buried under the oak tree in the grounds of Headley Court will do something. They won't know until they look that she's been there for seventy-odd years. And she was an RAF nurse so she'll have ID on her somewhere."

Jack smiled at his friend; he didn't tell him that confirmation of Mike's experience would set his own mind at rest as to his mental state. He simply nodded his agreement.

"Pay phone in the village. No time like the present." He downed the remainder of his pint, "Race you."

Mike gave his name as John Peters and told the desk sergeant that he'd seen a body of a young woman being buried under the oak tree at Headley Court. Then he put the phone down and wiped the phone clean with the sleeve of Jack's coat.

"Thanks," Jack said with a grimace, "That's cashmere."

"No problem." Mike looked intently at his friend. "Thanks, Jack. You could have just told me I was imagining it. That I was having hallucinations or something. You could have just dismissed it as PTSD - the doctors probably would have. I owe you."

"Yeah, you owe me two pints and the cleaning bill for my coat. Come on, you look knackered, let's get you back."

Mike had been back in bed only minutes when he saw the reflection of the blue lights in his window. But it was much later when the forensic team had excavated the unmarked grave and exhumed the body of the young nurse. Everyone was talking about it then. How she had been found with her skeletal hand clutching the identity tags of an army officer that had been wounded in Aden and how rumour had it that the forensics had shown that she had been strangled. Her body was reduced to bones after so long in the ground so that was all they could say officially. They said she was to have a military burial.

He made the decision then. If this was part of him then he would embrace it. He would study parapsychology and the paranormal and in so doing he may be able to do something useful, something to help himself to understand what was happening to him and possibly help others, living and dead. Suddenly his future didn't look so bleak.

She came to him again that night. "Thank you," she said, before she faded into the semi-darkness of his room.

GRIMALKIN COTTAGE

Mike Travis's day had started as any other, in other words - he was bored. His studies into the paranormal had taken him to a new understanding of what was happening to him and he'd had a few forays into practical work investigating some routine phenomena. He had no idea that as he downed the third cup of coffee of the day that events were going to propel him into a whole new ball-game.

The post had dropped through his letterbox and a cursory look told him that it was all bills, until he leafed through them and came to the last one in the pile. It was a handwritten envelope with a Preston postmark. He opened it expectantly and was not disappointed.

Dear Mr Travis,

I saw your recent advertisement offering paranormal investigation services and hoped that you may be interested in something that has happened to us recently.

As you will see from my address, Newchurch in Pendle, I live in Lancashire in the area renowned for the famous, or infamous, Pendle Witch Trials. Before I proceed, I need you to know that I am far from given to fanciful ideas about witches or haunting but recent events have shaken my unbelief.

My wife and I recently moved into a cottage on the outskirts of the village which was built in 1804 and therefore should have no association with the dark history of the area. We have only lived here for six months and prior to our purchase the cottage had been empty for fifty years or more and was in a derelict state. It is now fully renovated and up until now has been a comfortable and happy home.

Recently, we have been disturbed by horrible noises in the night, ranging from screams to howling. Our dog won't come into the cottage and my wife has been suffering from depression and more recently has

17

developed a horrible skin disease.

The landlord of the local pub tells me that the cottage had been built on the site of Malkin Tower which was once the home of Elizabeth Demdike, the leader of the Pendle Witches.

Are you interested in helping us?

Yours in hope

John Stokes.

Was he interested? Did the Pope eat fish on a Friday?

He called the number at the top of the letter and after speaking to John Stokes he packed his car with his equipment and headed for Lancashire.

Mike had quickly developed his own rules for investigations and was constantly adding to them with experience. Rule No. 1: Treat every investigation on its own merit, with a healthy scepticism and open mind. Rule No. 2: Look for normal everyday reasons for any phenomena first.

The letter had mentioned howling and growling and that the Stokes' had a dog which wouldn't come into the cottage. Every reason for it to howl and growl in the middle of the night. Also the cottage was located in an area where the wind howled from off the Pennines and a faulty chimney or flue could provide the sound effects for any Hammer Horror movie. As for the mysterious skin disease; stress could be a safe bet as the cause of it.

The Forest of Pendle, and in particular Pendle Hill, has long been known as witch country and the mention in the letter of Elizabeth Demdike set his investigative juices flowing. She had been the supposed leader of the coven of witches that had been tried and hung in 1612. And Malkin Tower, a cottage in fact, and not a tower, had been the home of Elizabeth Demdike and long since demolished into history. It was also purported to be the meeting place for the coven to perform their evil magic. This was going to be interesting.

The journey was tiring and painful as his leg always

caused him great pain after a long drive, but he didn't stop for rest, wanting to get to the cottage in the shortest time possible. He tossed pain killers down his throat and continued on.

Grimalkin Cottage looked inviting in the warm light of the setting sun and John Stokes came quickly from within to greet him.

He was extremely thin and looked to be in his sixties with a harrowed expression and dark circles under his eyes. Mike swiftly ascertained that the cottage had been bought in anticipation of a peaceful retirement, which had proved far from reality. He felt immediately sorry for the man. John told him that his wife was staying with their daughter as her nerves just weren't up to being at home, and that he was going to join her to leave Mike free to carry out his investigation. He left almost immediately.

So far, Mike's investigations had been into fairly benevolent hauntings and a strange poltergeist with a fixation for pulling up carpets. He instinctively knew that this was going to be something else. Something he hoped he was up to.

He checked the chimney and flue and all seemed to be in order. An inspection of the pipes and plumbing showed no obvious defects and in any case he'd switched off the central heating to rule out air in pipes. The cottage was small, and so setting up his microphones, computer recording equipment and cameras with night vision lenses took no time at all and he settled down to watch and wait.

Around one-thirty he began to notice a chill descend over the entire cottage and despite having a warm jacket he found himself shivering. The noises were subtle at first, soft knocking sounds from the main bedroom, then footsteps from behind him, footsteps that sounded like feet on stone steps. Stone steps that weren't there.

He was on high alert then, holding his breath but previously he'd been able to see in the cold air. It was so cold that his leg was in supreme agony from the devastating injury he'd undergone after his helicopter crash with the resulting surgery and the insertion of a scrap-metal-dealer's dream. It always played him up when he was cold. He ignored it.

When the howling and growling began he decided it was time for a reality check. The Stokes' dog had left with his master so couldn't be implicated. What the hell was he doing there? This was a far cry from shadows on a wall and ripped up carpets. This was the heavy stuff.

The cottage, already dark, became a black cavern and the last embers of the fire died as suddenly as a light switch turning off. From beside the fireplace the darkness seemed even denser. A black shape was forming, and it was beginning to move.

He heard the soft whirr of his computer and recording equipment and the motion sensor on his camera clicked into action. The black shape came closer.

His military training took over and the discipline kicked in as the black shape took on the appearance of an old woman. Suddenly, her face was right in front of his and the smell that came from it made his stomach turn. A combination of noxious potions and unwashed body assailed his nostrils, and God alone knew what prevented him from retching.

But he was in this for good or ill and he was going to do what he was being paid for - investigating the phenomena.

"Who are you?" he demanded with as much authority as he could muster.

The reply was a harsh and discordant laugh that brought goose pimples to every inch of his skin. When the laughter died away he heard the word 'Demdike' and then came muttering, indistinct at first, then settling into a steady rhythm.

Realisation brought defiance. The old bitch was casting a spell.

"Enough of that! What do you want, Demdike?

Elizabeth isn't it? Why are you plaguing these people? You don't belong here!"

There was silence for a moment, and then the laughing came again, followed by the low muttering. An image came unbidden of holding out a cross in front of himself like something he'd seen in a cheesy movie, and he couldn't stop the laugh that broke from his lips.

It evoked a loud hiss from the old woman and the muttering got louder; he'd really pissed her off. Rule No. 9: Don't provoke them!

It was muck or nettles now. "Tell me what you want!"

She mocked him then in a whining childlike voice, "Tell me what you want!"

He carried on. "I'm not leaving and neither are the good people that live here. This isn't your home any more. Go back to whatever hell you've come from."

He'd done it again, stomped all over Rule No. 9! He really needed to get a grip on that.

Elizabeth Demdike leaned even closer to him and it took all his resolve not to back off. Too late he saw the pin in her hand that she plunged deep into his left thigh. He couldn't prevent the scream of agony as the pain shot through him like a red hot poker being shoved into the site of his injury.

This was new. Physical interaction with a spirit was something he'd believed impossible. New rule. Rule No.27: Nothing is impossible.

"What do you want?" he demanded again when he'd regained his breath.

She began to circle around him and it took every ounce of inner strength to remain calm and not to move. He daren't let her see that he was inwardly shaking. She began to speak in a sing song voice that reminded him of fingernails on a blackboard.

"Ding dong bell," she chanted.

Pussy's in the well.

Who put her in?

Little Johnny Thin.
Who pulled her out?
Little Tommy Stout.
What a naughty boy was that,
To try to drown poor pussy cat,
Who ne'er did him any harm,
But killed the mice in the farmer's barn."

Mike was puzzled, "What does that mean?"

"Ding dong bell.
Pussy's back in the well.
Who put her in again?
Little Johnny Thin again,
Who pulled her out?
No-one was about.
So poor pussy drowned this time
And so I say 'Revenge is mine!'"

Mike stared at the old woman, "Is this about a *cat*?"

"My cat! My Grimalkin! Drowned in my well while I was out in the fields. But he paid then and he'll pay now!"

Mike's mind was doing somersaults, trying to make sense of the rhyme. Johnny Thin ... John Stokes? He was certainly thin. Did she believe he was the culprit come back to the scene of the crime? Could it be that simple?

She came in closer still and hissed at him. "And my well was poisoned and they filled it in. I want it back! Only then will I give them peace!"

"And that's it? You want your well back? Then you'll leave them alone?"

"Perhaps, and perhaps not. I loved my cat."

"You do know that the man who lives here is not Johnny Thin?"

"Who says so? Eh? Who are you to say? Eh? What do you know? I know! Oh, yes, I know. And before long, he'll know!"

"What if they give you back your well?"

"Maybe, maybe not."

She seemed to grow smaller all of a sudden, changing back into the black shape that retreated to the fireplace again. Embers that had died in the hearth sprang back into flame and the cottage seemed warmer, lighter.

Mike hit the rewind button on the sound recorder and heard only white noise. His video camera with night vision had picked up and recorded the black shape that resembled a bent old woman, but that was all. His thermometer was stuck at zero and had refused to change with the returning warmth. Instinct told him that the action was over for the night, so he packed his equipment back into his car and made himself comfortable to wait for morning and the return of John Stokes.

At nine, the pre-arranged time, John Stokes pulled up outside the cottage. He looked refreshed, having spent the first peaceful night for months. "Well?" he asked.

Mike had been considering his response for the last few hours and he knew what he was going to say.

"Was there an old well on the property when you moved in here?"

"Yes. It was damned dangerous so I had it filled in."

Mike nodded, "You may want to dig it out again and make sure it's kept clean and fresh. I think that may solve your problems."

John Stokes looked at him as if he were deranged. "Is that it? That's all you can come up with?"

Mike's initial liking of the man began to fade. "That's it. You asked for my investigation and its outcome and that's it. You can take my advice or leave it. It's up to you, but if I were you I'd take it. I've left the bill for my expenses on your coffee table."

John Stokes was obviously not satisfied but that was his problem. If he took the advice, Mike was sure their problems would disappear. He walked to the door and turned back briefly.

"Do you like cats, Mr. Stokes?"

"No! I do not! Nasty, sly creatures. I hate them!"

"Thought so. You'll maybe want to rethink that too," he said as he got into his car.

THE MISTLETOE BOUGH

When Mike Travis was invited to investigate Barnwell Hall in Hampshire, he was delighted. His study into the paranormal had included many written reports of unexplained phenomena and this magnificent Jacobean mansion, now a girl's boarding school, had always intrigued him.

The snag was, he had read the reports and the history so often that he felt he already knew the place. This ran contrary to what he liked to call, 'Travis Rules'. Rule No. 1: Treat every investigation on its own merit, with a healthy scepticism and an open mind. He knew that would prove difficult given his enthusiasm for the Hall and its long-dead occupants.

And now, the telephone call from one of the House Mothers had awakened the cherished desire to go and see it for himself.

His research into the history of Barnwell Hall had shown that it had once been known as Mistyldene, being the Old English name for Mistletoe, and owed its name to the abundance of the mystical plant that grew in the ancient oak tree at the front of the house. Superstition of times past had caused one of the owners to rename it and he, along with subsequent owners, had been responsible for the sympathetic restoration of the entire building.

Mistyldene had been mentioned twice in the Domesday Book, the earliest references of the house went back as far as Edward the Confessor and the Hall still boasted an ancient gateway and cellars of the original fourteenth century building.

There were reports of several ghosts on the premises but the lasting and enduring legend was one of The White

25

Lady. The origin of the legend was a young bride, Alys Fitzherbert, who on her wedding day, hid inside a carved chest with a hidden spring that could only be operated from the outside. No-one had found her and everyone assumed that she had been run away. Instead, the poor girl had suffocated, and her mouldering corpse was only discovered long after she struggled for her last breath, still clutching a sprig of mistletoe. It was said that the mistletoe on the oak tree died that day too, never to return.

Since then the apparition of a young woman dressed in white and carrying a sprig of mistletoe, had often been seen in the upstairs corridor where the chest had rested, and each time that she had been seen there was an overpowering scent of lily of the valley. Mike had often wondered why she would have hidden in the chest on that of all days, or why no-one had heard her muffled cries for help. Assuming there had been any. His sense of the macabre had provided several explanations, none of which were conducive to happy thoughts.

The House Mother, a rather anxious Mrs. Allerdyce, explained that some of her girls were being woken in the night by the sound of weeping, and the sight of what they had described as a woman in white. The apparition had always been accompanied by an overpowering fragrance of lily of the valley. The Headmaster, she said, strongly disapproved of her contacting him, believing it would only serve to aggravate the situation. But he was away at a conference for the following week, it being half-term, and most of the girls would be at home or on holiday. She needed him to be discreet. There was to be no published report of his investigation.

He agreed. Actually, he would have agreed to sever one of his toes if it meant the chance to investigate Barnwell Hall. He reminded himself of Rule No.1.

The approach to the Hall was through the fourteenth century arched gateway of sculpted stonework and red brick. It immediately gave the feeling of stepping through into another time. That was dangerous as far as the investigation went; Mike needed to stay focussed on the present and on any paranormal activity that he may or may not witness during his time there.

At the top of the gravelled drive, Barnwell Hall rose spectacularly from open parkland. Its red brick and carved stone edifice told of a time when kings and queens were frequent visitors, and carriages not cars, would pull up outside the flight of stone steps that led to the dramatic entrance. Mike felt humbled by the sheer beauty of the place. Again he chided himself to keep his thoughts in neutral.

A thin woman appeared at the top of the steps and hurried towards him. She had a pinched face, with horn-rimmed spectacles perched low over her thin and pointy nose. She wore a long cardigan that seemed to catch the breeze, and she reminded Mike of a flapping hen. That seemed entirely appropriate to him; she was after all a House Mother whose job it was to fuss and flap over her charges.

There were only half a dozen girls remaining over half-term, she said, and they had been relocated to another wing of the Hall for convenience. The affected area of the Hall would be entirely at his disposal. He would kindly keep to that corridor and not venture into the opposite wing where the girls were temporarily housed. A request he readily agreed to; the thought of hysterical girls running around terrified him more than any malignant spirit.

Inside, the Hall was no less impressive than outside, with its wide sweeping staircase that gave way to two identical corridors. He looked at Mrs. Allerdyce for confirmation. She understood his quizzical expression immediately; she was obviously used to reading people. "To the left," she said sharply.

"Thanks. I take it you are aware of the Hall's history, dating back to when it was known as Mistyldene? I can't help feeling that name suited the place better. More romantic."

Mrs. Allerdyce sniffed loudly. "Romantic nonsense and not conducive to a place of learning. Now, if you will excuse me, I have to attend to my girls." She hurried away leaving the impression of a frantic hen trying to round up her straying chicks. Mike liked her immensely.

His investigation was to be restricted to one corridor only and so his preparations and setting up of his equipment was straightforward quickly accomplished. He briefly thought about having a look around but the image of the flapping hen chasing him made him reconsider. There was a comfortable chair at the end of the corridor which gave an excellent view of the entire area. He settled into it with his laptop and couldn't resist browsing the history of the place once more.

The time passed swiftly and it was soon dark. He checked the night-vision camera again and his voice recorder. His laptop was now connected to his equipment. He sat and waited.

The change in the atmosphere was subtle at first, producing a prickling sensation down his spine and a fluttering in his stomach. Signs that he was beginning to recognise as his body's warning system of impending paranormal activity. The fragrance came then, delicate at first, but soon there was an overpowering scent of lily of the valley. He stood up, ready for whatever was about to happen. Subtlety was not the characteristic of the weeping however, which when it came, echoed around the corridor in heart-rending sobs.

She was beautiful in her white lace wedding-dress with its long train, and her ebony hair was covered in a veil of finest linen. But there was the unmistakable look of terror on her face as she looked around frantically, as if searching for something. Or for somewhere to hide.

What happened next would categorise the manifestation as a 'recording' or replay to which he could only be a spectator.

There was movement on the stairs and Mike saw a large man with a hooked nose and the expression of a snarling dog. He was clearly not one of the nation's starving, with ripples of fat constrained under a black velvet doublet and a white ruff at his throat. The pale pantaloons he wore were also stretched to their limit and forced into knee-high black boots. His hard face was accentuated by a close-cropped beard and moustache. He was bounding up the stairs in long strides, roaring at her to get back to the bedchamber and submit herself to her marital duty. Alys Fitzherbert looked terrified as she clutched the mistletoe bough to her chest, still frantically searching for a place of safety. Mike felt sickened and more than helpless, knowing he could do nothing but watch events unfold.

A second before Fitzherbert reached the top stair, she threw herself into a huge carved chest that Mike had not previously noticed; in fact it hadn't been there. Fitzherbert was in the corridor then and entered each room one by one, looking angrier every time he emerged. Eventually he gave up and disappeared back down the stairs.

The whole thing began again, with loud and copious weeping, but now as Alys cast about for somewhere to hide, the carved chest was nowhere to be seen. The scene repeated itself over and over, until Mike suddenly realised that he was witnessing a message. She needed the chest to conceal herself! Eventually the apparition faded into the ether, along with her weeping, ready to return again on another night when the drama would be endlessly repeated.

He knew what he had to do.

His recording equipment had done its job, and the heart-rending laments were captured well. They ripped into him as he listened to them again, only too well aware now of their implications. The apparitions had made no impression on his video recorder, but a white mist pervaded the entire corridor on the film. There was no evidence, either sound or video, of the poor girl's brute of a husband.

At five in the morning, Mrs. Allerdyce came to him and spoke in a hushed whisper. Her girls were asleep but she had heard the commotion, being awake in the first room of the opposite wing.

"I think I know what may help," he said to her in equally hushed tones. "You need to find a large wooden chest, large enough for someone to hide inside. I suggest though, that you keep it locked to prevent one of your girls from doing so and then being unable to get out again." He knew that a lock would not prove a problem for the girl who could pass through walls. He guided her to the spot where he had seen the chest. "Just here," he said gently.

"I expect there will be something in one of the attics," she said. "I'll find some excuse for its removal to the corridor. Please remember that discretion in this is very important. If the headmaster finds out, I will be in extremely serious trouble. I think I can trust you?"

He smiled at the worried, flappy woman and rested his hand on her bony shoulder. "You can trust me," he said. He couldn't resist a quick peck on her cheek which resulted in the reaction he'd expected as Mrs. Allerdyce flushed wildly and hurried back to her chicks.

It didn't take long for him to pack up his gear and he left the corridor feeling wistful, and hoping to the core of his being that the new chest would provide shelter for Alys Fitzherbert. It was time she found peace.

He was thoughtful all of the way home, wondering over again what other phenomena would come his way. He couldn't help feeling that this one would never have a truly happy ending, but then not all stories did.

Back in his living room, that was also his study and his library and temporary storage area, he opened his laptop case and gasped.

Tucked neatly at the side of his laptop was a bough of Mistletoe.

THE SOLDIER'S RETURN

Mike Travis frowned at the growing heap of papers on his desk, grimacing at the pile; it was way past time to clear it.

Clearing his desk to Mike usually meant throwing everything into the waste bin. He gave a second glance at the glossy brochure, proclaiming the delights and luxury of the Plas Derwyn Hotel in West Wales that he'd been just about to discard as junk mail. Then the thought briefly crossed his mind that such mail usually arrived on his computer screen, not his doormat, so he gave it another look; it had, after all, been addressed to him personally.

The front of the brochure showed an attractive Georgian house set on a cliff with stunning views across Cardigan Bay, and inside the triple-fold brochure, Mike found a note taped across a photograph of an oak panelled bedroom with a four-poster bed. He carefully peeled it away. It was a brief invitation from the proprietor to carry out an investigation at his hotel and a telephone number to call if he was interested. There was no further information but the note ended with the offer of a free stay at the hotel if he took the case.

He'd been busy recently working on a television series with one of the satellite networks, which had been a huge commitment but would ensure that whilst not rich, he would be comfortably off for the foreseeable future. He was tired, so the offer of a free stay in a posh hotel appealed to him. He shrugged; there was nothing to lose in making the call.

The hotel, it seemed, had a 'problem'. Every year on the same date there were disturbances at night; it had been that way ever since Gareth Jones and his wife had bought the place seven years ago. Gareth, as he insisted Mike call him, was reluctant to specify the disturbances, but he said they were bad enough to warrant closing the hotel to guests at that time each year. He and his wife lived and slept in the annexe at the back of the house and Mike would be the sole occupier during his investigation. The lack of information didn't worry Mike; sometimes it was better that way as he couldn't form any opinion prior to the investigation. The trouble was due to occur in two days time, on October 30th, not really short notice as the brochure and the enclosed note had been on his desk for a couple of weeks. He decided to go.

The brochure hadn't done justice to the hotel, which stood in splendour, high on the cliff in beautiful grounds, reflecting the late-autumn sunshine from its white frontage. Inside was equally welcoming, and Gareth ushered him into a tasteful and comfortable lounge where coffee and cakes were waiting for him.

Greetings and formalities over, Mike settled back into the sumptuous sofa; he hadn't felt this relaxed for a long time. He enjoyed the moment, not wanting to be too relaxed for the night vigil.

Still with no idea of the nature of the annual disturbance, and not wanting to know the details he settled into a general discussion with his host.

"It isn't unusual for manifestations to appear on the anniversary of a death, or a specific traumatic incident. The emotion of what happened can imprint itself into the atmosphere and replay itself on that date or time. I can't explain the mechanics of it at the moment, but it isn't an unusual occurrence. What is unusual, is the fact that it affects several of your guests at the same time. One or two sensitive people being affected wouldn't surprise me, but if as you say, the problem is bad enough to close the place, it has to be a pretty strong manifestation. Let's wait and see what happens."

Gareth left Mike early so that he could set up his video camera and voice recording equipment in the room that seemed to be the focus of the disturbance. It was obvious at first glance that it was the luxurious room featured in the brochure, and that it was the last room in the corridor and the biggest. A door in the wall opposite the bed opened into a huge bathroom the size of his living room. Two massive Georgian windows looked out onto the neatly clipped lawn and the bay beyond, and Mike was pleased he wasn't paying the bill. He looked forward to his promised week's freebie later in the year.

Around eleven he switched off the lights and settled into the armchair under one of the windows.

The hotel was absolutely silent, even the central heating made no sound, but it was a restful silence, and the knowledge that he was alone in the house was something he was well used to. The armchair was too comfortable and around two- thirty he did the unthinkable in the middle of a vigil, and drifted into a light sleep.

It didn't last long however, as he was jolted awake by a loud banging coming from the far end of the corridor that sounded like someone hammering on a door. He stood to go and look, and as he did so the banging sounded on every door in the corridor. His own included. He wrenched it open, and saw only the dimly lit corridor lined with firmly closed doors. He stood outside his room and waited for a repeat performance, but wasn't gratified.

As he re-entered his room he took an involuntary step backwards.

The entire room had changed, even his equipment had vanished. In sharp contrast to the room he had just stepped out of, it had taken on a feeling of gloom. As he looked around he noticed that the bathroom was no longer visible, due to the wall having disappeared - and the room was now twice its original size. In the far corner, a free-standing mirror cast dark reflections into the room.

Almost filling the space between the two windows two large framed sepia photographs had appeared. One was the head and shoulders of an army officer, the other a pretty young girl sitting next to a table. Mike stepped up for a closer look. Under the serious but handsome young officer's face the words *Captain Thomas Evans December 1915* had been printed. Underneath the photograph of the young woman were the words, *Rebecca, August 1916*.

Below the photographs, against the wall, was an occasional table covered in heavy lace on which was laid a newspaper, 'The Daily Herald', dated November 8th, 1916. The front page was dedicated to an article predicting victory in the Somme, confirming that despite the horrendous casualties, many regiments were coming home.

By the side of the newspaper was a telegram, the contents of which said, "Regret to inform you Captain Thomas. E. Evans killed in action France October 30th". Mike knew better than to try and pick it up, this was definitely a replay of the recording type of manifestation and there would be no interaction with the participants.

As he stood there wondering who had received the devastating news, his question was answered. Through the door stepped a young woman, whose grief was so deep there were no tears. She passed by Mike without acknowledgement and dropped a large card on top of the telegram. Looking over her shoulder, he could see it was an invitation to a wedding that would never take place. It said simply, Colonel Richard and Mrs. Dorothy Wells cordially invite you to the wedding of their daughter, Rebecca, to Captain Thomas Evans on December 1st, St. Margaret's Church, Cardigan. R.S.V.P.

An overwhelming sense of sadness permeated the air and lodged in Mike's chest. This was going to be an investigation that he could not participate in, and therefore be of no help to either the living or the dead.

As he watched, the scene changed, and to his surprise Rebecca appeared through the door again, but this time she was wearing a high- necked wedding dress of heavy cream lace, to which was pinned a mourning brooch over her left breast. She wandered to the mirror and stood looking sadly at her reflection, and although Mike was beginning to feel like an intruder, he felt compelled to stay. He stood behind her, and was unsurprised to see that his reflection was absent from the mirror. He was after all, glancing at a moment in time long past.

What did surprise him however was Rebecca's reflection, which faded and reappeared in a parade of images. In each one she wore her wedding dress, and in each one she looked older. And thinner. The wedding dress changed from cream to brown and began to hang on her almost skeletal frame. Her face became sallow and wrinkled, until it eventually looked like parchment, dried and dusty. Mike watched as her life simply wasted away, her dress hanging in a tattered web, until her image became a very old woman, still wearing her wedding dress and brooch, and who now lay dead before the mirror. He was about to turn away when the door opened again, and Thomas Evans entered and walked across to the mirror. Reflected in the glass, Mike saw the handsome young officer tenderly bend to kiss his beautiful bride, who stood next to him, young and radiant in her wedding dress.

He couldn't check the tear that rolled down his cheek as he hung his head. Two more victims of a pointless war. He could call himself Squadron Leader and relax in the Officer's Mess, they all could, but he was just as much a victim as they were. They were all victims. Innocent puppets of the political machine. When would the world learn? The truth was that it wouldn't. But he would do what he could for other innocent victims and try to help them find closure. The living and the not.

He couldn't remember a time when his investigations had left him feeling so sad, and so emotional, and he realised that this probably wouldn't be the last time that he'd witness past grief intruding on the present. It was what it was. Rule No. 30: You can't win them all.

But he'd have a damn good try.

In the morning he packed away his equipment and

went in search of Gareth. There was a welcoming smell of bacon and eggs and coffee emanating from somewhere behind the dining room. He followed the tantalising aroma, and pushed open a door which took him into the kitchen. Gareth looked up at him expectantly. His expression said, 'Well, what happened?'

Mike gave him an exact account of the night's events.

"What can we do?" he asked Mike.

"Just let them be. I suggest that if you and your wife take a holiday, take it at this time, and give them some space. Do what you do and close for the night. I'm sorry I can't be of any more help to you, but there is nothing else I can suggest."

"Shall I call in a priest?"

"You can if you want, but for the sake of one night, I'd be inclined to let them have their reunion."

Gareth nodded. "I think you're right. After all, what's one night in the year?"

Mike said that he didn't feel he could accept the free week's stay as he hadn't been able to do anything practical to help, but Gareth insisted. "Come in the summer," he said. "I'll make sure you have a different room."

Mike smiled at him and accepted the offer. After the hearty breakfast he took a slow and thoughtful drive home. He needed another case to come his way soon, something he could get his teeth into, something that he may be able to be of practical help with.

He picked up the single letter from the doormat and tossed it onto the table. He was hungry and in pain from his leg after the drive, and knew his cupboards resembled those of Mother Hubbard. There was some stale bread and the remnants of a jar of marmalade, and no milk in his fridge. Toast and marmalade with black coffee and painkillers it was then.

He read the crabbed handwriting in the letter over his second breakfast. It hadn't taken many minutes for him to become intrigued, and he made the decision to respond before his coffee and painkillers had kicked in.

He looked again at the date of the original postmark. It had taken almost two months to find him, eventually forwarded to him by the television channel that had produced the series about paranormal phenomena in which he had regularly appeared. Since his RAF helicopter crashed in Afghanistan and left him with enough metal in his leg and chest to cause havoc at airports, and to be of actual value on the scrap-metal market, he had lived on his generous pension and a few articles on the paranormal. It was the articles that had brought him to the attention of the television director, and he hadn't looked back. In an effort to find proof of the paranormal, he inevitably ended up debunking it or uncovering a hoax, or worse a deliberate fraud. Sometimes he'd been able to help the living, sometimes the dead. Now his interest had been grabbed by the letter.

Two hours later, he was in his black Volvo estate heading down the M5 motorway for the tiny village of Crowsmoor, in Cornwall, and whilst he could find no such village on any map, he had reasonable directions from the old man who had written the letter.

He puzzled over the contents as he drove.

*'Problem is I'm getting very tired and frail. I don't know how much time I have left. That's the problem. Who'll ring the bells when I'm gone? It has to be a member of my line. **Has to be**. Understand? It's always been the eldest male in my family. That was the agreement. There's only me now, and I turned ninety two this April and I'm feeling weary, I knows my time is near. So, who'll ring the bells when I've gone? And none as matters knows that I'm gonna be gawn soon, 'cept the Good Lord above. Then what will they do? Every morning at six and every evening at six. Six tolls of the bells. The bells have to be rung dead on six; otherwise . . .He'll come back.*

*The dead don't sleep quiet here in Crowsmoor, they never have. Not since **he** came, anyway. Must be four hundred years gone now.*

Folk round here close their eyes to it. Don't understand see. They think that when I've gone they can maybe get someone else to ring the bells, or they won't bother being as they believe its naught but owd superstition and they'm being too modern to think on it. They hear them, everyday, they hear them, but they don't understand. They don't understand what the bells keep away. Or they don't want to know. Tho' there's mebbe a few that does for other reasons. But I know. Last of the line now I am though, so who's going to ring the bells when I'm gone? No-one, that's who, and then they'll understand.

Saw you on the telly I did, on that programme about the supernatural. Thought to myself, 'He might understand.' so I'm writing to you for help. You can't ring the bells. No-one can, but you might be able to stop what will happen when they bain't rung.

I hope you come in time. I want to explain everything to you. What will happen? I hope you don't think I'm just a mazed old man, rambling. God knows, it's the truth.'

And Mike knew the truth when he heard it.

And don't forget to sign up for my newsletter for details of my latest books and a FREE short story!

http://janmcdonaldemailsign-up.gr8.com/

THANK YOU!

To my Reader:

Many thanks for buying *Beginnings*, I hope you enjoyed reading it.

If you did enjoy it, please post a review at Amazon, Goodreads or your favourite social network site and let your friends know about *Beginnings*.

I hope that this has whetted your appetite to read the other novels in the Mike Travis paranormal investigation series. You can find details of these in the next few page as well as the other short story collections.

Happy Reading!
All the best
Jan

ALSO BY JAN MCDONALD

Mike Travis Paranormal Investigations
The Crowsmoor Curse: getBook.at/Crowsmoorcurse

Long Shadows: getBook.at/longshadows

The Sacred Ark: getBook.at/sacredark

The Haunted Diary of Victoria Little:
getBook.at/haunteddiary

The Merlin Manuscript: getBook.at/merlin

The Sin Eater: getbook.at/sineater

Mike Travis short stories
Halloween: getBook.at/halloween

Christmas Spirits: getBook.at/christmasspirits

The Beckett Vampire Trilogy
Midnight Wine: getBook.at/midnightwine

Lycan: getBook.at/lycan

Part 3 coming 2015

ABOUT JAN MCDONALD

Jan lives close to the Welsh borders which have their own mystical quality and provide endless resources in the way of legends and folklore surrounding paranormal experiences. She loves all things paranormal and has read the best: Dennis Wheatley, Stephen King, Edgar Allan Poe, Bram Stoker and all those authors that excel in the creepy or downright scary world of paranormal events.

When she embarked on the Mike Travis series, she realised that the field of paranormal investigation is more than we see on the popular TV programmes. So in order to provide compelling ghost hunting tales but with the greatest accuracy, Jan trained as a Paranormal Investigator and has studied parapsychology.

CONTACT DETAILS

Visit the authors website:
    jan-mcdonald.co.uk

Follow on Twitter:
    www.twitter.com/janmcdonald1

Cover designed by: Raven Crest Books

Published by: Raven Crest Books
    www.ravencrestbooks.com

Follow us on Twitter:
    www.twitter.com/lyons_dave